POGMAN™ DISCOVERS AMERICA

By Shane DeRolf • Illustrated by Mitch Schauer

Colorist: Ruben Huante • Cover design: Dave Silva • Art director: Cheri Brewster

Random House **New York**

Copyright © 1995 World POG Federation. All rights reserved under International and Pan-American Copyright Conventions.
Published in the United States by Random House, Inc., New York, and simultaneously in Canada by Random House of Canada Limited, Toronto.
POG logo, characters, names, and all other elements are trademarks of World POG Federation.
Library of Congress Catalog Card Number: 95-68711
ISBN: 0-679-87825-4 Manufactured in the United States of America

10 9 8 7 6 5 4 3 2 1

nce upon a tropical island, far from the civilized world, there lived a simple-minded ball of fur named Pogman and his best friend, a purple cat named Pogpuss.

Pogman was always busy doing something. He loved to explore the island in search of new things to show his best friend.

4

Pogpuss kept busy, too. He loved to explore the island in search of new places to hide from his best friend.

Together, they had lots of fun.

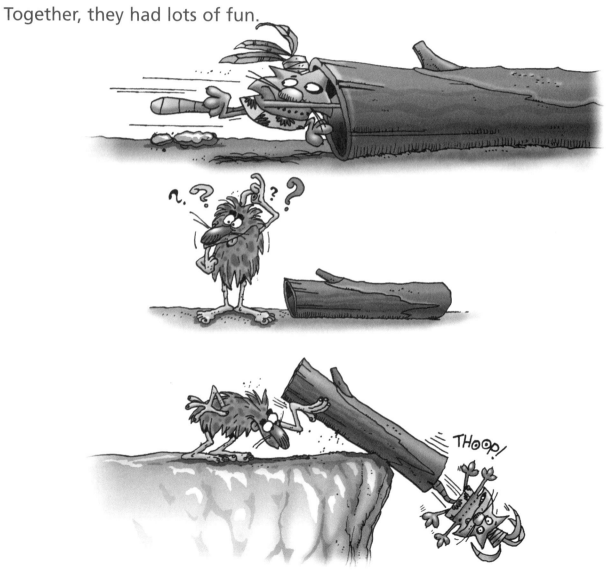

One day a message arrived in a bottle...
a *milk* bottle.

Pogman wasn't much interested in the message, but he absolutely *loved* the milkcap.

Pogpuss, on the other paw, read the message.
The message was...

And it was.
Never doubt a message in a milk bottle.

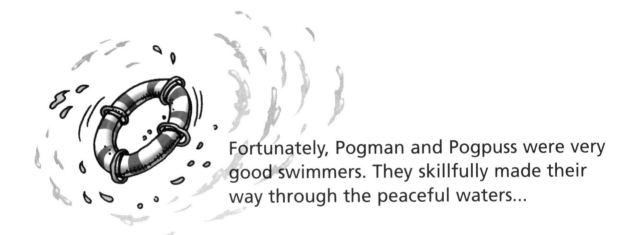

Fortunately, Pogman and Pogpuss were very good swimmers. They skillfully made their way through the peaceful waters...

And gracefully embraced mainland culture.

"Welcome to Muscle Beach," said Mr. Lifeguard. "You dudes local?"

Pogman scratched his head. He had no idea what Mr. Lifeguard was saying. In fact, Pogman wasn't even sure what Mr. Lifeguard was.

You see, Pogman had never seen a human being before...
let alone one who spoke English.

"What's the matter?" asked Mr. Lifeguard.
"Cat got your tongue?"

No such luck, thought Pogpuss as he prepared for the worst.

"Uh-oh," said Pogpuss.
"Now we're *really* in trouble."

And they were.

"Nice monkey," said Pogman as he reached out to pet Mr. Lifeguard, who just happened to be standing in front of a sign that said: DON'T PET THE LIFEGUARDS!

After a short but interesting visit to California, Pogman thought it might be fun to learn more about this strange new land called America.

Pogpuss, who couldn't agree with him less, looked around for a place to hide.

But learning about America can be pretty tricky, especially if you're a simple-minded ball of fur that thinks a honking truck is a friendly duck...

...and that the middle of the intersection is a good place to ask for directions...

...and that *all* little old ladies want to be helped across the street...

...and that it's *always* better to give than to receive.

Despite all these wonderful experiences, Pogman still loved America. It was an exciting new place filled with interesting creatures, unusual customs...

...and some of the sweetest dreams that a little orange furball could ever have.